THE
KREE-SKRULL WAR

By Thomas Macri

Illustrated by Ramon Bachs *and* Hi-Fi Design

Based on the Marvel comic book series The Avengers

MARVEL

New York

marvelkids.com

© 2013 MARVEL

Published by Marvel Press, an imprint of Disney Book Group. No part of this book may be reproduced or transmitted in any form or by any means, electronic or mechanical, including photocopying, recording, or by any information storage and retrieval system, without written permission from the publisher. For information address Marvel Press, 1101 Flower Street, Glendale, California 91201.

SUSTAINABLE
FORESTRY
INITIATIVE

Certified Chain of Custody
Promoting Sustainable Forestry

www.sfiprogram.org
SFI-01415

The SFI label applies to the text stock

Printed in the United States of America
First Edition
1 3 5 7 9 10 8 6 4 2
G658-7729-4-12061
ISBN 978-1-4231-5406-8

If you purchased this book without a cover, you should be aware that this book is stolen property. It was reported as "unsold and destroyed" to the publisher, and neither the author nor the publisher has received any payment for this "stripped" book.

Chapter One: Avengers No More!

Captain America, Thor, Iron Man, and the Hulk might be the most famous Avengers. But they aren't the only Avengers.

Once, the core Avengers were away. Other members were on duty. A friend of the team's was in trouble! They were in New York City. He was in Miami. They rushed to their Quinjet to find him.

Among them was Vision. He was an android who could walk through walls. Quicksilver could run really fast.

Scarlet Witch had a hex power to make anything go her way. Hawkeye's eyes were as sharp as a hawk's. His arrows never missed their targets.

Their friend was Captain Mar-vell.

He was a Kree alien from another
world. He had been stuck in a different
dimension. He took on a lot of dangerous
radiation there. The Avengers needed to
help their friend. They arrived in Miami
and found him. But Mar-vell didn't
know he was in danger. He thought the
Avengers were trying to attack him. So
he fought them.

The Avengers knocked out their
friend to keep him from fighting them.

They brought him to a special lab.
They hooked him up to a machine. The
machine took away the radiation.

Soon, the public found out that there was an alien on Earth. They thought he was here to hurt them. A senator named Craddock wanted people to hunt down the aliens. But the team didn't turn over their friend, Mar-Vell.

Instead, they sent him away to hide.

People became angry at the Avengers. They thought they were traitors to Earth. The core group of Avengers arrived at the mansion. Captain America, Thor, Iron Man, and Hulk told Vision, Scarlet Witch, Quicksilver, and Hawkeye that they had disgraced the name of the Avengers. They said that they were breaking up the team—forever!

Chapter 2: The Avengers Return

The Avengers' Mansion was quiet and empty. And then a few days later Vision returned. He stormed into the mansion.

He was surprised to find Thor,
Iron Man, Captain America, and Hulk
inside. Why were they here? They had
broken up the team! Before Vision
could ask, he fell to the ground.

The Avengers didn't know what was wrong with him. They called Ant-Man and Wasp to help. They were Avengers, too.

Ant-Man and Wasp rushed to the mansion. They shrunk down. They were so small they could fit into the Vision's mouth. Then they went inside the android!

Being inside the Vision was like being in another world. The Super Heroes were attacked by strange things. These things seemed to have a mind of their own.

Finally, Ant-Man and Wasp made their way to Vision's brain. They were able to fix him. Ant-Man knew that he and Wasp had to escape before Vision woke up. If they didn't, Vision's body would attack them!

They made it out of the Vision just
in time.

Vision woke up. The other Avengers asked where his teammates were.

Vision explained that they had been taken captive by a crew of aliens called Skrulls. Vision blamed the core Avengers for this. After all, they had broken up the team. They had sent him and his three teammates on their way.

But the other Avengers had no idea
what he was talking about. This could
only mean one thing. They knew the
Skrulls could change the way they
looked.

It must have been Skrulls pretending to be the Avengers! They were the ones who sent away the others. The team checked their security recordings to prove it. The Avengers needed to save their teammates!

Chapter Three: Battleground Earth

But first they needed to find them.
They needed any information they
could get.

They learned that the Skrulls were at
war with the Kree. They were the two
strongest races in the universe. Earth
was halfway between the Kree and Skrull
worlds. This made it a very valuable
prize. Whichever race controlled Earth
would have a strategic place in the stars!

To make matters worse, the Kree's good leader, Supreme Intelligence, was being held captive. The evil Kree ruler, Ronan, had him locked up. Ronan ruled the Kree. Ronan loved war.

Meanwhile, on board a Skrull spacecraft, Scarlet Witch, Quicksilver, Hawkeye, and Mar-vell were held captive. The Skrulls thought that these heroes could be used to help them take Earth. They wanted to use Mar-vell. They wanted him to create a Kree weapon for them.

They tried to fool Mar-vell. They told him that the Skrulls would free his friends if he helped.

Back on Earth, Craddock was still trying to get people to hate the Avengers. He also wanted the people of Earth to hate any alien. It didn't matter if the alien was good or bad. People were listening to him.

Things had never been worse for the Avengers.

Chapter Four: War!

Then, things began to change. The core Avengers and Vision located the Skrull station where their friends were held. They rocketed off in their Quinjet.

Halfway there, the Avengers found Ronan. He set an army of Kree warriors against them. The Avengers fought hard, and won.

Now the Supreme Intelligence could once again rule the Kree in peace. No longer would they wage war against the Skrulls.

But the Kree were only part of the
problem. The Avengers continued
their voyage. Then their ship came up
against a huge fleet of Skrull vessels.

The Skrulls attacked
the Avengers.

The Avengers battled right back. They were only a few of Earth's mightiest heroes. They were fighting the most powerful army in the universe. Still, against all odds, the Avengers made it to the Skrull space station.

Meanwhile, Captain Mar-vell was working on his Kree weapon. Or, at least that's what the Skrulls thought. The Skrulls came to check on him. Mar-vell smashed the weapon. He freed his friends. And the battle began.

The team was together again at last.
The battle was long. The Avengers
fought hard.

Finally, they won! The Kree were now free from Ronan. The Skrulls were weakened. Peace had been restored.

The Avengers' work was done. They said good-bye to Mar-vell. They headed back to Earth.

44

Chapter Five: Home

The Avengers were welcomed home to cheers. The people of Earth loved them again. What had happened?

The Avengers learned that Craddock was actually a Skrull pretending to be a human! He was put on Earth to start trouble. When the people of the Earth discovered this, they locked him up. He was in a special jail. He couldn't ever escape.

The Earth was safe for the Avengers once more. And the Avengers had once again made the universe safe for the people of Earth!